For all the really good dads

A todos los muy buenos papás

G. P. PUTNAM'S SONS
An imprint of Penguin Random House LLC, New York

Visit us online at penguinrandomhouse.com

Library of Congress Cataloging-in-Publication Data
Names: Gee, Kimberly, author, illustrator. Title: Mine, mine, mine, yours! / Kimberly Gee. Description: New York: G. P. Putnam's Sons, [2021] | Summary:
Illustrations and easy-to-read text portray a busy toddler playdate full of playing, taking turns, sharing, and more. Identifiers: LCCN 2020044063 (print) |
LCCN 2020044064 (ebook) | ISBN 9780593112403 (hardcover) | ISBN 9780593112427 (kindle edition) | ISBN 9780593112410 (ebook) | Subjects:
CYAC: Play—Fiction. | Friendship—Fiction. Classification: LCC PZ7.G2577 Min 2021 (print) | LCC PZ7.G2577 (ebook) | DDC [E]—dc23
LC record available at https://lccn.loc.gov/2020044063 | LC ebook record available at https://lccn.loc.gov/2020044064

Manufactured in China
Special Markets ISBN 9780593531167 | Not for resale
10 9 8 7 6 5 4 3 2 1
RRD

Design by Marikka Tamura | Text set in Neutraface 2 Display | The art was drawn in pencil and painted digitally.

This Imagination Library edition is published by Penguin Young Readers, a division
of Penguin Random House, exclusively for Dolly Parton's Imagination Library,
a not-for-profit program designed to inspire a love of reading and learning, sponsored
in part by The Dollywood Foundation. Penguin's trade editions of this work are
available wherever books are sold.

MINE
MINE
MINE
YOURS

MÍO
MÍO
MÍO
TUYO

Kimberly Gee

Traducción de **Ariela Rudy Zaltzman**

putnam

G. P. PUTNAM'S SONS

Come in,
come in,
come in...

Entren,
entren,
entren...

go out!
¡salgan!

Hide, hide, hide…
Escóndanse, escóndanse, escóndanse…

find.
encuentra.

Stop,
stop,
stop...

Para,
para,
para...

go!
¡sigue!

Over,
over,
over...

Encima,
encima,
encima...

under.
debajo.

Jump, jump, jump...

Salten, salten, salten...

bump!
¡chocan!

Sorry, sorry, sorry.
Perdón, perdón, perdón.

That's okay.
Está bien.

Mine,
mine,
mine...
Mío,
mío,
mío...

yours.
tuyo.

Yours,

yours,

yours.

Tuyo,

tuyo,

tuyo.

Mine!
¡Mío!

Messy, messy,
Sucio, sucio,

messy...
sucio...

clean up.

recojan.

Bye,
bye,
bye,
bye,
bye...

Adiós,
adiós,
adiós,
adiós,
adiós,
adiós...

BYE!
¡ADIÓS!

Come again!

¡Vuelvan pronto!